It was summer and the sun
shone down on a cricket,
who leapt and skipped about.
“What fun!” he cried, as he landed
beside a bee. “What are you doing?”
“Collecting pollen,” replied the bee, “to
make food to store in our hive.”

“Food to store?” said the cricket. “Whatever for? What a silly Bee,” he added in a whisper as he leapt off.

From morning until evening, he continued to have fun, jumping and hopping about, and singing happy, summery tunes with his long, back legs.

Next morning, the cricket sat looking on as some ants rushed back and forth, collecting seeds and carrying them back to the anthill.

"What are you doing?" said the cricket. "Collecting food and storing it for the winter," the ants replied.

The cricket scoffed at them. "You silly ants!" he cried. "Look around you. There is plenty of food. Winter will not come for a long time, so why not just have fun like me? Let me entertain you with a tune," he offered, and he used his long, back legs like a fiddle to make a merry tune for them.

"No, thank you," said the ants. "We must collect as much food as we can, or else we will starve in the long winter."

"What silly ants," muttered the cricket, and he shook his head as they marched off. He just did not understand why everyone was so boring.

All summer long, the cricket continued to have fun. There was still plenty of food about and he did not see the point of bothering about winter yet.

"Morning, bees," he'd call and wave. "Morning, ants. Haven't you finished all that storing yet?" and he'd shake his head at them.

Then, one morning, the weather started to get chilly.

“Winter will be here soon!” cried the cricket. “I suppose I had better start collecting some food.”
But when he looked around, there was not much food left.

He collected a small store of seeds and hid them in a hole in a tree. "That will do," he muttered. "I do not need much food in winter and I can look for some more if I run out."

As the winter went on, the weather got colder and colder, and the cricket felt more and more unhappy.

"I am too cold to sing," he said sadly, as he sat shivering. "It is so cold that I am all out of tune."

Then, one morning, he woke up feeling very hungry. He helped himself to a seed and sat and ate it, shivering. It did not fill him up, so soon he stretched out his arm for more, but his hole was empty. He had used up all of his store of seeds!

All this time, the ants had been snug and happy under the ground. They still had plenty of food left, and they were planning a party. They had sorted out some party games, but there was still something missing.

"We need something to listen to!" they said.

Just then, one of the ants remembered the cricket who had offered to amuse them in the summer.

“Perhaps he will come and entertain us,” they said, and some of them set out to look for him.
“Brrr!” they said and shivered.
“It is freezing out here.”

When the cricket spotted the ants,
he hid from them.
"They will see that all my food has gone," he said to himself. "Then they will blame me for having fun all summer instead of collecting food like they did.

"Cricket! Cricket!" called the ants, but the cricket kept hidden, sadly waiting for them to go. Then, just when they were about to give up, one of the ants spotted him.

The cricket was thrilled to go with the ants into the snug nest and to join the party. The ants gave him a big plate of food and he was so happy that he fiddled tunes for hours. But when the party was finished, he looked sadly out of the anthill at the wind and rain outside.

"Thank you so much for having me," he said humbly, as he got ready to go. "It was a good party."

The ants looked at the cricket and then around at the snug nest.
"Cricket, why not spend the rest of the winter down here with us?" they said.
"We will give you food if you will entertain us."

The cricket smiled and nodded happily.

So, for the rest of that winter, the cricket lived underground with the ants. He was no longer lonely, freezing, and hungry. Instead, he had lots of friends, a snug bed, and plenty of food until summer came around again.